Tears of a Friend

I turn to Claire. 'What do you think?'

'Hang on a minute,' she says. 'Do you think this makes me look fat?'

'No,' I say, 'but look at me!'

She glances at me. 'It's all right.'

She's looking at herself again.

I'm suddenly angry. 'Look properly!' I say loudly.

Claire looks surprised. And a bit annoyed. But she *does* look at me.

'Yeah, it's nice. Bit revealing though, isn't it? For you, I mean.'

Look out for other exciting stories
in the *Shades* series:

A Murder of Crows by Penny Bates
Blitz by David Orme
Gateway to Hell by John Banks
Hunter's Moon by John Townsend
Nightmare Park by Phil Preece
Plague by David Orme
Space Explorers by David Johnson
Treachery by Night by Ann Ruffell
Who Cares? by Helen Bird

SHADES

Tears of a Friend

Joanna Kenrick

Evans

Published by Evans Brothers Limited
2A Portman Mansions
Chiltern St
London W1U 6NR

First published in 2004

British Library Cataloguing in Publication Data
Kenrick, Joanna
Tears of a friend. - (Shades)
1. Young adult fiction
I. Title
823. 9'2 [J]

ISBN 0 237 52731 6

Series Editor: David Orme
Editor: Julia Moffatt
Designer: 'Rob Walster

Chapter One

'It's just not fair,' says my best friend Claire.
'Parents are so mean. Midnight isn't late.
I mean, not *really*.'

I look at her. Claire is fourteen, the same
age as me. But unlike me, she's pretty. No,
not pretty. *Gorgeous*. She has this long
blonde hair. It's silky and shiny, like in the
adverts. Mine is short and boring brown.

She flicks her hair while she talks. It makes her look like a model and boys love it. I tried to flick mine once, too. Mum thought I had nits.

'You're not listening, Cassie! They've grounded me for a *week*!'

I stop thinking about Claire's hair. 'Sorry. But didn't they say you had to be in by eleven?'

'Whose side are you on?' Claire snaps. 'You know I had to go to Nick's gig.' (Nick is her older brother. I fancy him rotten but I wouldn't ever admit it. Even under torture.)

'Was it good?' I ask.

'Brilliant. There was this gorgeous bloke there—'

I knew it. I bet she snogged him.

The school bell rings. We pick up our bags.

'Oh by the way, did you know Louise is having a party?' says Claire.

Suddenly I feel very excited.

'Really? When?'

'Next Thursday. It's a sort of well done party for her sister.'

'What for?'

'She passed her driving test at last.'

We grin at each other. We don't like Louise's sister. We found it very funny when she failed three times. Ha ha ha!

'But will your parents let you go?' I ask.

'Who cares? I'm going anyway. I'm fed up with being treated like a child. Can't wait 'til I'm sixteen.'

'Me too.'

'They won't be able to boss me around then.'

By this time we are sitting down in class. It's maths with Mr Price. We laugh at him a lot. When he gets embarrassed the back of his neck goes red. Our class embarrasses him a lot on purpose. We sent him a valentine's card from the geography teacher. We knew he fancied her. His neck stayed red for forty-five minutes. I know because I timed it.

When the bell goes, Claire says to me 'God, maths is boring, isn't it?'

'God, yeah,' I say. Actually I quite like maths. But of course I can't say that.

'I was thinking about Louise's party,' says Claire. She sighs. I know what's coming. 'I've got nothing to wear.'

We always go through this. Claire's wardrobe is twice the size of mine. She has loads of really nice shoes too. I counted mine the other day.

I have:

Two pairs of trainers

Three pairs of sandals (two with sand in, one that gives me blisters)

One pair of 'smart' shoes for school
One pair of 'cool' shoes with heels
Oh, and one pair of wellies.

I have also grown out of my one decent dress. Not upwards, just outwards.

'I've got nothing to wear either,' I say.

Claire cheers up. 'Let's go shopping!'

'Okay. How about two o'clock tomorrow?'

Chapter Two

Next day is Saturday. There's a new shopping centre near me. It's got Top Shop and Miss Selfridge and all the really good high-street stores. There are some funky little boutiques too. You can find really unusual stuff in them: camouflage clothes and flares. We've been coming here since it opened a few months ago and I always spend too much money. Not that I get much of an allowance.

I look around at the crowds of people. The centre is always packed on a Saturday.

'Over here, Cassie!' calls Claire. She is looking stunning as usual. Pink crop-top and tight jeans. And—

'Oh my God!' I gasp. 'Have you had your belly-button pierced?'

'Fooled you!' giggles Claire. She shows me the little sparkly jewel. 'It's stick-on. I bought it just now. Claire's Accessories.' She winks. 'So good they named it after me!'

'It looks really cool,' I say. Now I want one too. But that would be copying. And my tummy isn't flat like hers. Maybe if I don't have dinner tonight?

'Come on, there's some new stuff in Top Shop.' Claire drags me off.

We have a brilliant time. I love trying

on clothes. Dresses, trousers, little tops, big baggy jumpers, short skirts – it's how I imagine heaven to be. One big shopping centre in the sky where you can shop forever.

We're in Dorothy Perkins. Claire has got this dress on that looks amazing. (Of course. I mean, she could wear a dustbin sack and look amazing.)

I'm pulling on a dark green velvet top. I gasp at myself in the mirror. I look *fantastic*. The top is very low cut. I have a cleavage.

I turn to Claire. 'What do you think?'

'Hang on a minute,' she says. 'Do you think this makes me look fat?'

'No,' I say, 'but look at me!'

She glances at me. 'It's all right.'

She's looking at herself again.

I'm suddenly angry. 'Look properly!' I say loudly.

Claire looks surprised. And a bit annoyed. But she *does* look at me.

'Yeah, it's nice. Bit revealing though, isn't it? For you, I mean.'

'What do you mean, for me?'

I can feel hot, red anger boiling up inside me.

'Well,' Claire shrugs, 'it's just not your style.'

I am furious now.

'And what exactly is my style? Looking boring, I suppose? Being covered up? Wearing last year's fashions? Wearing the cheap versions of *your* clothes? Oh, *I* know what my style is. It's just anything worse than yours. To make you look better when you stand next to me. Well thanks a lot!'

As I pull the green top over my head I hear a seam rip. I don't care.

'See you around, Claire,' I say. She looks

really silly, her mouth hanging open as she stares at me. I storm out of the changing room. I fling the top at the shop assistant.

'No thanks,' I say. 'It's not my *style*.'

What an exit!

I am very impressed with myself. To start with. But after about five minutes I begin to feel really down. When I get home I burst into tears. I'm angry with myself and with Claire. After a while I'm not angry any more, just sad.

Maybe I can make it up with Claire tomorrow? But why should I? She should say sorry first.

I fall asleep with a headache.

Chapter Three

Monday at school is a nightmare. Mr Price tries to make us work together on a problem. I haven't seen Claire since Saturday.

'I'd rather not work with Cassie, if you don't mind,' says Claire. She won't look at me.

'All right then,' says Mr Price. I can tell he's surprised.

I pretend not to mind, but something inside hurts.

At break-times I have no one to talk to. Claire and I hang around all the time together. I've never needed any other friends. Now I wish I'd made the effort.

Every time Claire walks past me she flicks her hair and looks away. I kind of hope she will come up to me. Say she is sorry and can we be friends again? But she doesn't, and I can't do it myself.

Over the next few days it's as though we were never friends at all. As though our history together never happened. I make friends with Isabel, the nerdy girl in the class. She's so grateful someone has finally talked to her. It makes me feel sorry for her. She has even less confidence than I do. It annoys me in a way. I wish she'd stand up for herself a bit.

Is this how Claire thinks of me?

Even Mum notices something odd.

'Where's Claire these days?' she says. 'I haven't seen her for ages.'

'We're not friends any more,' I say.

She doesn't ask again.

The day before the party, I decide something. Maybe it's time to make some changes. Maybe Claire's right, in a way. I should make more of an effort with myself, the way I look. Maybe then I'd have more confidence, be more popular.

I go back to Dorothy Perkins and buy the green velvet top. The one with the ripped seam is still on the rail. I choose a different one, hoping none of the shop assistants recognise me.

Watch out world! The new improved Cassie is about to break loose...

Chapter Four

On the night of the party I should feel
excited. Instead I just feel nervous and sick.
Normally Claire and I would get ready for
a party together. We would spend hours
making ourselves look beautiful. Well,
she would look beautiful. I would look
sort of okay.

I nearly decide not to go. But then I feel

angry. Why should Claire stop me having a good time? Most of the people I know from school will be there. I can have a good time without her.

And her gorgeous brother Nick might be there too…

I pull on the dark green velvet top. I'm right, it does make me look amazing. I decide to wear a short black skirt and my heeled shoes. I wish I had knee-length boots, but I've spent my allowance for this month. As usual.

I spend ages on my make-up. I'm not very good at it yet. We're not allowed to wear it at school. I practise at weekends but I still haven't got the hang of eye-shadow. I usually put too much on and look like I've got two black eyes.

There's not much I can do with my hair. Whatever style I try, it always ends up looking a frizzy mess. I put loads of mousse in it. It does look quite nice but it feels horrible, like stiffened glue.

I'm finally ready.

'You look nice,' says my mum.

'Thanks.' I wonder if she means it. She doesn't like me wearing short skirts. Maybe she's just being nice.

'Honestly, who has a party on a school night?' she says, shaking her head. 'Why couldn't it be tomorrow? None of you will be in a fit state for school in the morning.'

I mumble something and open the front door.

'Hang on, I'll walk you to the party,' calls Mum, pulling a coat on.

Horror!

'No, Mum! Honestly, I'll be fine.'

How embarrassing – what if anyone sees me?

'Look, I'm not letting you walk in the dark all the way there. I'll walk you to the corner, okay?'

'Mum…'

'It's not up for discussion, Cassie. Here, put your coat on.'

'No thanks, I'll be fine.'

'It's cold out.'

She's right, but there's no way I'm wearing my school coat to the party.

'Don't nag, Mum.'

'All right, freeze to death. See if I care.'

We set off. In less than a minute I have goose-pimples. But I can't rub my arms to keep warm. Mum will say, 'I told you so.'

At the corner of Louise's road, she stops. 'Have a good time then, snowman.'

'Thanks,' I say through chattering teeth. My feet are starting to hurt too. The shoes rub my heels.

'No later than eleven,' she says. 'And get someone to walk you home, or call me.'

'Yes, Mum.'

I leave her at the corner. I know she'll watch me until I reach Louise's house. It annoys me a bit, but I'm also secretly glad.

As I reach Louise's front door, I hear a shout to my right.

'Hey, Cassie!' It's Isabel. I almost die of shame. I didn't realise she was coming. We haven't talked about it. I didn't think it would be her sort of thing.

But here she is, tottering along in four-inch heels. She looks ridiculous. She's wearing a sort of fishnet top over a black vest. Her hair is back-combed and piled on top of her head. And she's even worse than me at make-up.

But it means I've got to go into the party with her. People will think that we came together.

Oh well. Better get it over with. I smile weakly at her. Then I ring the door bell.

Chapter Five

It's not Louise who opens the door. It's some boy I don't know.

'Hi,' he says. His eyes are kind of red. 'Come in.'

Isabel and I step into the hall. There's loud hip-hop music coming from the front room, but there's a huge crowd of people in the way. I shrink back against the wall.

'Come on!' calls Isabel. 'The fun's always in the kitchen!' She bounces off, pushing her way through the crush. I stay where I am.

There are a lot of people here I don't know. Louise's sister must have invited them. Most of them seem a lot older than me.

Then my heart stops. It's Nick, Claire's brother. He's wearing a leather jacket and holding a cigarette. He looks *amazing*.

'Hi,' I blurt out, before my brain can stop my mouth. 'I'm Cassie, Claire's friend.'

Nick turns to look at me, and then – I can't believe this – *I put my hand out*. To shake hands with him. How stupid is that?

'Oh yeah, hi,' he says, although I can tell he doesn't recognise me. He ignores my hand, and I snatch it back quickly.

'How are you?' I burble. 'I hear your gig went really well last week.'

Nick stares at me.

'Yeah, it was cool.' He takes a swig from a beer bottle. His eyes slide down. 'Nice top,' he says. Then he pushes past me and goes into the front room.

My hand goes automatically to my neckline to try to pull it up a bit higher. I should feel pleased that he liked my top, but weirdly I feel a bit dirty. I didn't like the way he looked at me, as though he could see right through my clothes. And I'm cursing myself for being so stupid. I mean, going to shake hands! My face burns with humiliation, and I head towards the kitchen, avoiding people's eyes.

'Sorry,' I say as I push past a couple snogging by the stairs.

'Watch where you're going,' snaps the girl. It's Claire. Her eyes open wide when she sees me. But then she pulls the boy's head towards her and starts kissing him again. It's not someone I know. I go past, feeling sick.

The kitchen is buzzing. There's a funny smell in the air too, like Mum's musk perfume. I pour myself a coke and try not to catch anyone's eye. This is worse than I thought. Why did I come?

'Hiya, gorgeous.' A boy with floppy dark hair nudges me with his hip. He looks about eighteen, and his eyes are fixed on my cleavage. I begin to wonder whether the top was a mistake. 'Want to have a bit of fun?' He dangles a little bag in front of my eyes. It looks like it's full of dried leaves. I frown.

'What's that?'

The boy grins. His blue eyes look really huge.

'It's heaven in a bag, baby.'

Then it hits me. He's offering me drugs.

'No thank you,' I squeak out. My face must show how horrified I am.

'Ah, go on. You look like the kind of girl who needs to relax.'

He's very tall, and leaning over me. I shrink back against the fridge. 'No,' I say, but my mouth has gone dry. His gaze drops again to my cleavage and he reaches out a hand. I don't know why but I'm completely frozen. My mind is saying *move, move!* But my body isn't listening. His eyes are hypnotising.

'Hiya, Cassie,' says a cheerful voice from behind the boy. 'Fancy some fresh air?' And a hand reaches round and firmly grasps my wrist.

Chapter Six

It's not until we're out of the kitchen that I start to breathe. I don't even know who's rescued me until he turns around and grins at me. White teeth in a dark face.

'Mark!' He's in my class at school but I don't know him that well.

'You looked a bit desperate,' he says, letting go of my wrist. He grins at me.

'Hope I did the right thing.'

'Yeah, thanks,' I say, my head spinning. My body is just waking up and it's feeling a bit wobbly.

'You don't have to go outside with me, that was just to get you away from that bloke.' Mark has to raise his voice as we head into the hall.

'No, I'd like to,' I yell. 'It's too hot in here.'

As we head out the front door, we pass a couple going up the stairs.

'Isn't that your friend Claire?' Mark says suddenly.

I turn. Claire is heading up the stairs, giggling. The guy she was snogging earlier is grabbing her bum as he follows her. Her skirt is practically up around her waist. My jaw drops.

'Somebody's got lucky then,' grins Mark.

I follow Mark out into the front garden.
The noise level drops, and I find myself
taking big gulps of air.

'Are you all right?' Mark looks at me in
concern. 'Sit down.'

I sink on to the garden bench with relief.
'I'm fine. Honestly.'

Mark sits down next to me and there's a
bit of an awkward pause. My head is still
reeling from the sight of Claire going
upstairs with a perfect stranger. But I'm
also beginning to wonder about Mark. Why
did he rescue me in the kitchen? Is he
expecting something in return? I sneak a
sideways look at him. He's nice, I guess, but
I don't really fancy him. Does he fancy me?
What do I do if he does? My head hurts.

'I hate parties,' Mark says suddenly.

'What?'

'Parties. I hate them. Everyone gets

dressed up in completely stupid clothes. Everyone tries to drink too much to show that they're really cool. Then you're expected to get off with someone you don't even like. Because otherwise you won't have had a "good time". It stinks.'

'I know exactly what you mean!' I say in relief. 'And what's so cool about throwing up all night?'

'Or getting slobbered over.'

'Or having to use the bathroom when there's no toilet paper and people have thrown up in the loo.'

'Or someone spilling drinks down your only decent outfit.'

We grin at each other.

'Why did we come?' Mark says in amazement.

'Because—' I start. 'I don't know.'

'I like being out here, though,' he says.

'Me too. We can watch everyone else making fools of themselves.'

'Excellent.' He produces a bottle of lemonade from behind his back. 'Want another really uncool drink?'

'Definitely.'

Chapter Seven

After that we get chatting really easily.
It's nice actually. I don't have any friends
that are boys (mostly because they're all
really stupid) but Mark's okay. And once
I've realised that he's not about to grope
me, or try to snog me, we get on
surprisingly well. We talk about school,
friends, family. I tell him about my row

with Claire and he seems really interested.

It must be about half an hour later when there's a commotion at the front door. Some girl comes running out really fast. Her face is all streaked with mascara and lipstick and she's got no shoes on.

It's Claire. She nearly trips on the paving slabs and I find myself going to help her.

'Claire, are you okay?'

She stares at me like she's never seen me before.

'Get off me, get off me!' she screams. She pulls away and stumbles into the road. I follow her.

'Claire, are you okay?' I can't think of anything else to say. Of course she's not okay, she looks awful. 'What's happened?' But she ignores me and hurries off down the road in her tights. 'What should we do?' I turn to Mark.

'Nothing,' he says, staring after Claire. 'You can't help someone who doesn't want to be helped. Does she live nearby?'

'Yeah, the next street.'

'Then she'll be home in a minute. She'll be all right.'

Thinking of Claire's wide staring eyes and tear-stained face, I'm not so sure.

Chapter Eight

It's only ten o'clock and Mum's surprised
that I'm home so early. She likes the look
of Mark though, I can tell.

'Thanks so much for walking her home,'
she says, looking him up and down. 'You're
in Cassie's class, is that right?'

I have to practically push him out of the
front door to prevent Mum asking him in

for a coffee. I mean, talking to Mark on my own is one thing. I'm not sure I want my Mum asking him questions about what his parents do, where he lives, all that. I think Mark understands. He gives me a wink as he goes.

'See you tomorrow, Cassie.'

'Yeah.' I give a bit of a grin, as if to say *aren't parents embarrassing?*

'You didn't have to be so rude,' Mum complains. 'I was going to ask him in for coffee.'

See? I knew it.

I make some excuse about being really tired and head off to my room. But it takes me ages to get to sleep. I keep thinking about Claire. I'm sure something's happened. I really hope she's got home all right.

She's not at school for registration. Or break. Or lunch. I'm so worried about her

I can't concentrate on anything. Mark
tries to talk to me in French but I'm so
busy thinking about Claire, I don't even
hear him, and he gets told off. I get yelled
at by teachers all day, and Mr Price gives
me detention.

When the detention is finally over,
I've decided what to do. I don't go home;
instead I go straight round to Claire's house.

Claire's dad opens the door. He works
from home.

'Hi, Cassie. We haven't seen you for a
while. Have you come to see Claire?' He
frowns. 'I hope you can be a good influence
on her. We caught her coming back from a
party last night. She was supposed to be
grounded.' He sighs.

'Oh,' I say blankly.

'I don't know what we're going to do.
She just doesn't listen to us any more.'

'She's probably just going through a rebellious phase,' I say, repeating what my mum has said a thousand times about me.

He nods. 'I guess so.' Then he seems to remember why I'm here and steps back from the door. 'Go on up. She's just got home from school.'

I glance at him, surprised, but decide not to say anything. He obviously doesn't know that Claire wasn't in school today. I make my way up the blue-carpeted stairs and try not to knock over the laundry basket at the top. I don't know why they put it there, I always seem to walk into it.

I hesitate outside Claire's door. She's got her 'Do Not Disturb' sign on the handle. We made them in Design and Technology at school. What if she doesn't want to see me? But I can't stand outside her door all evening, so I knock and go in.

'Claire? It's me.'

Claire is lying on her bed, knees drawn up to her chin. She's got her back to the door.

'I knew it was you,' she says shortly. 'I'm surprised Dad let you in, seeing as he's in a right mood with me.' She doesn't turn round, so I gingerly sit on the side of the bed.

'Are you okay?' I ask. 'Only, when you weren't in school today...'

She sits up at this.

'Ssh, keep your voice down. I would have stayed home but Dad would have pestered me all day, so I pretended to go out as usual.' She's wearing her school uniform, I notice.

'Where did you go?'

'What do you care?' She glares at me. 'I thought you were fed up with being my shadow? Copying my style?'

'I was,' I say hotly. 'But that doesn't mean I don't still care about you. I was worried.' I feel really cross with her. I've come all this way to see her (well, all right, a few minutes out of my way) and she's acting all huffy. I stand up. 'But if you'd rather I just butted out and left you to wallow in your own misery, then have it your way.' I turn to go.

'No, Cassie, wait!' Claire scrambles to the edge of the bed. I stop. 'Don't go, Cass. I need to talk to someone. Please.' She's sitting on the bed now, and her eyes are welling up. 'I have to tell someone.'

I walk back to the bed. 'Go on then. What happened at the party?'

She takes a deep breath and looks at the floor.

'That boy – he tried to – you know, Cass. He tried to make me have sex with him.'

Chapter Nine

I guess my face must show what I'm feeling, because she quickly says, 'Honestly, I'm all right. Really. I was just a bit shaken up, that's all.'

'You'd better start from the beginning.'

'Well, you saw me with that guy by the stairs,' Claire says. I nod. 'I met him about an hour before you showed up. He seemed really nice, said he went to school with Louise's sister. In Year Thirteen. Anyway, he seemed to really like me, and I didn't have anyone to talk to. I mean, normally I'd have talked to you...' She trails off.

I know what she means. But I don't want to talk about our argument. It seems pointless, silly now.

'It doesn't matter,' I say. 'Go on.'

'Well, I couldn't believe that he was really interested in me. I mean, he was nearly eighteen, and he was gorgeous. He could have had anyone. He said his name was Pete. I told him I was sixteen.'

'Claire!'

She looks sheepish. 'I know, but I thought he wouldn't be interested if he knew I was fourteen. Anyway, he started kissing me, and it was really nice. I was a bit nervous to start with but I got the hang of it. And he kept getting me drinks, which helped. I think he put something in the coke, because I started to find everything really funny. And then he said, "Do you want a tour of the house?" and I just thought that was hilarious.'

I groan.

'I know, I know,' Claire sighs, 'but you don't think about it at the time. I just got a bit carried away. Anyway, he took me upstairs.' She stops and takes a deep breath. 'It wasn't a tour, of course, he took me straight into a bedroom. But I didn't notice at the time because he was still kissing me and telling me I was gorgeous. Then I sort of tripped over, and we both fell on the bed. I was laughing so much I didn't think much of it, but then he started touching me. Putting his hands up my skirt and stuff.' She shudders.

'What did you do?'

Claire looks at me, her eyes big and swimmy.

'I didn't know what to do. I just sort of lay there for a bit, trying to move his hands away. And then I thought, maybe I should let him – you know – because I had been snogging him. And I did like him, sort of. Maybe I'd been leading him on. I shouldn't have snogged him in the first place. I should have said no right at the beginning, not halfway through.'

I shake my head.

'No, no, you can say no at any point. That's what my mum always says.'

'But when he realised I wasn't going to let him,' says Claire, a tear falling down her cheek, 'he said I owed him, that he couldn't stop now. Boys weren't built like that or something. You know, once they got started they couldn't stop.'

I stare in horror. 'That's not true, is it?'

'I don't know. I just kept pushing him away, but he was so much stronger, Cassie. I couldn't do anything. I was struggling and I think I was yelling but it's all a bit of a blur. I thought I was losing, Cass, I was getting really tired fighting him off. And then—' Claire gulps and takes a sobbing breath. 'Then Louise came in.'

Chapter Ten

'*Louise?*' I say in amazement.

'Yeah,' Claire smiles shakily. 'She went ballistic. Turns out we were in her parents' room. She was yelling about us being disgusting and didn't we have any respect?'

I let out a giggle. I can't help it.

'What did Pete say?'

'I don't know,' Claire says. 'He was

trying to find his trousers.'

I start giggling properly.

'His trousers?'

'Yeah. I just grabbed my bag and ran out.' Claire grins. 'Last I saw, Louise was whacking him over the head with her mum's box of tissues.'

We look at each other and burst out laughing. We laugh and laugh and roll on the bed clutching our sides. I can't tell if it's laughter or tears really – I think we're laughing instead of crying.

Claire's dad pops his head in to see what all the noise is about.

'Good,' he says, smiling. 'Glad to see you two have made up.'

We laugh even more at this, partly because who would have thought such a horrible event could bring us back together? I'm still thinking about Louise whacking some seventeen-year-old with a tissue box, and Claire is just laughing because she can't stop.

In the end, we calm down, just letting out the occasional giggle. We lie on the bed together and look up at the ceiling.

'Are you going to tell anyone?' I ask.

'Like who?'

'I dunno, the police or something. Shouldn't you tell your parents?'

'Are you mad? After the fuss they made when they caught me last night?'

'Well,' I say lamely. 'He might do it again. To someone else.'

Claire thinks for a minute. 'No. It must have been me. I got myself into that mess. If I'd just been firmer from the start…'

I look at her, but I don't know what to say. It can't have been her fault, can it? She was dressed – well, she was wearing a really short skirt. She wanted the attention, didn't she? But inside my head, I can hear my mum saying, 'Whenever you say no, it means no. Whatever you've said yes to before. No means no.'

'You told him to stop,' I said. 'You were fighting him off. He knew what he was doing was wrong. It's not your fault.'

I can't seem to find the right words, but I know inside that I'm right. It's all so complicated.

'Oh, it doesn't matter now,' sighs Claire. 'We were both drunk. He didn't manage to do anything anyway. I made a mistake. I'll know next time.'

There's a pause as we both stare at the ceiling again.

'So anyway, what about you?' Claire asks finally. 'Did you have a good time at the party?'

I grin. 'I met this boy…'

'Cassie!'

'Nothing happened,' I say, flapping my hand. 'Actually, it was Mark from our class.'

'Mark? The one who sits at the front in Geography?'

'Yeah. He rescued me from some creep in the kitchen who was trying to give me drugs or something.'

Claire's eyes open wide. 'Drugs? To *you*?'

I grin. 'I know, I know. To tell you the truth I was so freaked out I might just have said yes.'

'No, no, Cassie, you've got it all wrong,' says Claire, sitting bolt upright on the bed. She pushes a pair of imaginary glasses up her nose and frowns at me. I know what's coming. We've done this particular joke loads of times. I add imaginary glasses to my nose too. Then we both frown at each other and hold out our right fingers.

'Just … say … no…' we intone to each other, wagging our fingers in time to the words. Then we burst out laughing again.

All the hurt from the last week is going away. Where there was a hole inside me, now it's been filled up.

'I was really lonely,' I say to Claire, half-seriously.

'No you weren't,' she says. 'You had *Isabel*.'

I feel a bit uncomfortable. 'She's not like you, though.'

Claire squeals with laughter. 'Did you *see* her at the party? What did she *look* like!'

'I know. I thought *I* was bad at make-up.'

'No, you looked really nice actually,' Claire nods. 'I liked that top you were wearing.'

I gape at her. She obviously doesn't remember that it's the same one I tried on in front of her.

'You said it was a bit revealing last time.'

'Last time?' Claire stares back at me. 'I haven't seen it before.'

'Yes, you have. I tried it on when we were in Dorothy Perkins together. You said it wasn't my style.'

'I don't remember saying that. You must have misheard me. It looks great on you.'

I open my mouth to argue, but something stops me. This is all so familiar. We've been here before. And I know that if I carry on with it, we'll end up having another row. And I couldn't bear that.

'Never mind,' I shrug. 'It doesn't matter. Fancy going out tomorrow?'

'Down the shopping centre?'

'I dunno,' I say. 'Why don't we go

somewhere else for a change?'

'Okay. What about the cinema?'

'Cool, there's this new romantic comedy out.'

'*Cassie*, they're so boring. I want to see the new action film with Vin Diesel.'

'But I hate action films. All that violence…'

Here we go again.

Look out for this exciting story
in the *Shades* series:

Plague

David Orme

My father's shop was in Aldersgate Street,
just a short distance from the apothecary's.
Cheapside was busy as we crossed it. Even
though it was now dark, people were busy
filling carts with furniture and valuables.

'Fear of the plague is spreading fast,'
muttered the apothecary. 'All who may are
packing up and fleeing the city – especially
the clergymen, and they are the ones who
are needed most.'

'And what of you, Master Coulter?' asked

Jasper. 'Do you not fear the plague? You are in contact with the sick every day.'

'Fear it? Aye, I do that, but not for myself. When I was a youngster, the same age as your brother here, I was struck down with plague, and my mother despaired of me. But, by God's grace, I recovered. And it is my observation, Jasper, that those who are stricken once are rarely afflicted a second time. Though why that should be, I do not know.'

We were soon at the small saddler's shop. My mother was at the door, wringing her hands.

'Oh, Master Coulter, thank the Lord you are here!'

She almost dragged the apothecary in through the door. In the small upstairs bedroom my father lay groaning and coughing. His face was dead white, and was lined with pain. His nightgown was smeared with blood he had coughed up.

My mother turned beseeching eyes on the apothecary.

'Oh sir, it can't be plague. Look, there is no sign of the buboes upon him. Please, tell me sir, it is not plague!'

The apothecary examined my father's eyes closely, then sniffed at the bloody phlegm around his mouth. He looked at his chest, which was covered with dark marks, almost like bruises.

'Alas, Mistress Harper, it is plague. Not all patients have the buboes. In some, such as your husband, the signs of it are the dark marks on the skin and the bloody phlegm. The result is the same. Madam, you must prepare yourself. Your husband is dying.'

Blitz - David Orme

It's World War II and Martin has been evacuated to the country. He hates it so much, he runs back home to London. But home isn't where it used to be…

Gateway from Hell - John Banks

Lisa and her friends are determined to stop the new road being built. Especially as it means digging up Mott Hill. Because something ancient lies beneath the hill. Something dangerous - something *deadly*…

A Murder of Crows - Penny Bates

Ben is new to the country, and when he makes friends with a lonely crow, finds himself being bullied. Now the bullies want him to hurt his only friend. But they have reckoned without the power of crow law…

Hunter's Moon - John Townsend

Neil loves working as a gamekeeper. But something very strange is going on in the woods… What is the meaning of the message Neil receives? And why should he beware the Hunter's Moon?

Space Explorers - David Johnson

Sammi and Zak have been stranded on a strange planet, surrounded by deadly spear plants. Luckily mysterious horned-creatures rescue them. Now all they need to do is get back to their ship…

Who Cares? - Helen Bird

Tara hates her life – till she meets Liam, and things start looking up. Only, Liam doesn't approve of Tara taking drugs. But Tara won't listen. She can handle it. Or can she?

SHADES

Look out for these new Shades titles

Plague - David Orme

The year is 1665 and plague has come to the city of London. For Henry Harper, life will never be the same. His father is dead, and his mother and brother have fled to the country. Now Henry is alone, and must find a way to escape from the city he loves, before he, too, is struck down...

Treachery by Night - Ann Ruffell

Glencoe, 1692

Conn longs to be a brave warrior, just like his cousin Jamie. But what kind of warrior has a withered arm? Then he finds a sword in the heather, and he learns to fight using his good arm. And when the treacherous Campbells bring Redcoats into the Macdonald valley, Conn is going to need all the strength he can muster...

Nightmare Park - Philip Preece

Dreamland... a place where your dreams come true.
Ben thinks it's a joke at first. But he'd give anything to be popular. Losing a few short minutes of his life seems a small price to pay. But a lot can happen in a minute. And Ben soon realises nothing in life should be this easy...

Tears of a Friend - Joanna Kenrick

Cassie and Claire have been friends for ever. Cassie thinks nothing will ever split them apart. But then, the unthinkable happens. They have a row, and now Cassie feels so alone. What can she do to mend a friendship? Or has she lost Claire ... for good?